Lily's
Red Shoes
of
Courage

Lori Stevic-Rust, PhD

Integrated Press

ISBN: 978-0-9981472-1-5

Illustrations by Blueberry Illustrations
Blueberry Illustrations is a world class illustrations
and self publishing company. The illustrators of
Blueberry Illustrations are recipients of various
awards and nominations. More than 350 books
have been illustrated and published by the
company and many more are in the making.
www.blueberryillustrations.com

To little girls everywhere who
step into their courage to stand
up for themselves and others

and to the women who showed them how.

"Oh, no, the dough is going to blow!" Nana Emily punched down the dough, laughing. She got there just in time, before the donut dough flowed over the sides of the big white bowl and onto the table.

Most grandmothers were serious and often smelled like bug spray. But Lily's grandma laughed a lot, made up silly words, and loved to bake yummy treats.

Every day after school, Lily went to Nana Emily's house. They would sit together at the tiny white table in the kitchen. It was nestled so tightly between the refrigerator and the counter that Lily had to slide under the table to get into her seat.

Then Nana would say something like, "We're just as snug as a plug in a jug," which always made Lily laugh. Nana could make anything funny.

With her hands
in the soft dough,
squeezing and pushing it back
and forth, Lily felt happy. She had
forgotten about her stomachache—
the one that started a few hours ago, in school.

The dough felt sticky and smooth. Then Nana
Emily placed her hands over Lily's, and together
they formed the dough into a nice, soft ball.

Nana Emily smiled. "Oh, Lily, I am
so proud of you. This dough is so nice."

Nana Emily's words made Lily's stomach tighten. She
looked down at the floor and pinched her lips together
trying to stop the tears from coming, but it was no use.

Lily tried to look at her grandma but she couldn't. "Oh,
Nana Emily," she said, looking at her hands, "you wouldn't
be proud of me if you knew what I did at school today."

Nana Emily moved the dough to the side and took Lily's hands into hers. "Tell me what happened."

"There is a girl in my class named Aleeza. My friend Molly was making fun of her today. Molly laughed at Aleeza's head scarf and said it was ugly."

Lily's face felt hot. "I laughed, too."
Lily's shoulders sank. "I didn't make fun of her head scarf or say any of the mean things that Molly said, but still, I feel terrible."
Lily remembered how hurt Aleeza looked when everyone laughed at her.

Gently, Nana Emily asked, "Why did you laugh?"

Lily finally looked at Nana Emily. "I worried that if I didn't join in, then my friends would be mad at me, especially Molly. I didn't want her to laugh at me, too, or maybe not sit with me at lunch."

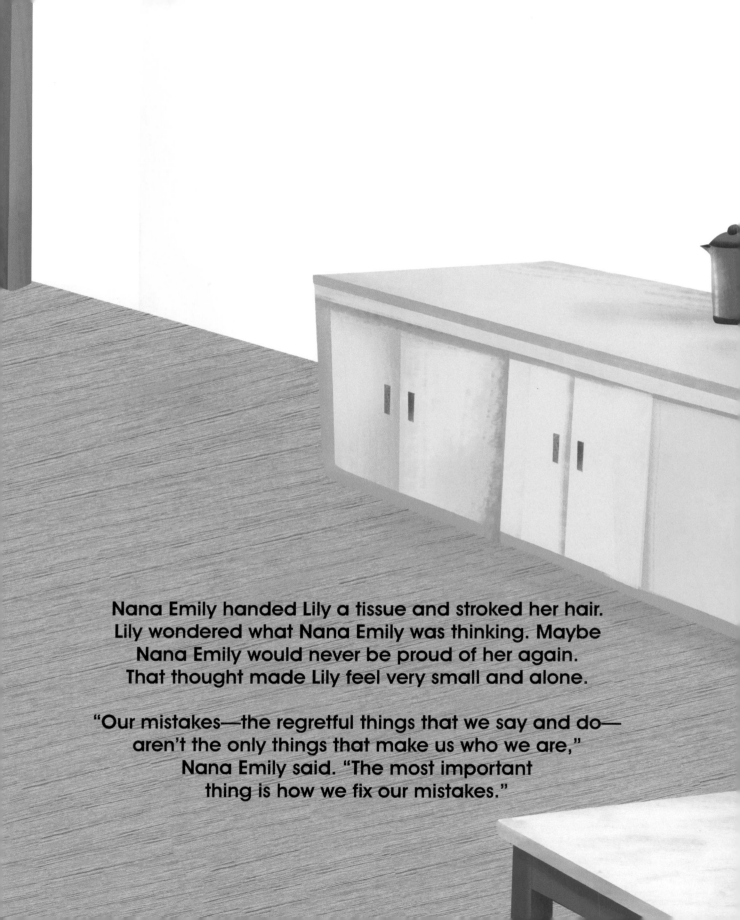

Nana Emily handed Lily a tissue and stroked her hair.
Lily wondered what Nana Emily was thinking. Maybe
Nana Emily would never be proud of her again.
That thought made Lily feel very small and alone.

"Our mistakes—the regretful things that we say and do—
aren't the only things that make us who we are,"
Nana Emily said. "The most important
thing is how we fix our mistakes."

Lily thought about how to fix her mistake.
She couldn't change that she had laughed.
Maybe, she could say she was sorry.

Lily tried to imagine apologizing to Aleeza.
She remembered other times when she had to
apologize for something she had done. It usually
made her face get red and her hands feel sweaty.
And it made her stomach hurt.

But after, she always felt better.
Nana Emily smiled at Lily. "Courage
to do the right thing, especially when
it is hard, is what gives us power."

"I want to tell you a story that I have never told anybody before," Nana Emily said in a whisper.

"When I was a little girl, I lived on a farm with my family. We didn't have much money for new clothes or shoes. When my older sisters outgrew their shoes, they would give them to me. By then, the shoes were usually dirty and had holes."

"At school, the other children would laugh at me and call me names. They would tease me about my old shoes."

"Sometimes I would ignore them and pretend I couldn't hear them. Other times, I would hit them with my metal lunch box. I would act tough," Nana Emily said with a sad face, "so that they wouldn't see that what I really wanted to do was cry."

"Then one day, I was walking home from school on my usual path through the woods. It was a fall day and colorful leaves covered the ground. The sun was shining on one pile of leaves, and something in that pile caught my eye. It was sparkling.

"What was it?" Lily asked, her eyes getting big.

"There, like they were waiting just for me, were the most beautiful pair of shiny, red shoes. And that's not all. The word *Courage* was written on them in sparkling, gold letters.

"I wondered who would leave such an amazing thing in the woods!" she said.

"I looked around, but I was alone—alone with the most beautiful pair of shoes I had ever seen in my life.

I wondered if they would fit me. I untied my old, dirty brown shoes with the holes and carefully slipped on the red shoes with the gold letters.

They fit! They were soft and comfortable, like a pair of warm slippers. I stood up," Nana Emily told Lily.

Nana Emily remembered how special she felt in those shoes. "I twirled. I danced. I laughed," she said with a giggle.

Lily was listening to her grandma's story with great interest. "What did you do then, Nana Emily?"

"Well," Nana Emily said, "I looked at my old shoes laying there in the dirt and then down at my feet in those magical red shoes. I wondered what my mother would think.

I wondered what the other children at school would think!

I couldn't wait to show them off! I threw my old shoes in my school bag, and I ran home."

"When I ran into the house, my mother looked
up from the pot she was stirring on the stove.
'Where have you been, Emily?
You are late, and I was starting to worry!'

"I lifted up my foot. 'Mother, look
what I found! Aren't they the most
beautiful shoes you have ever seen?"

"My mother looked down at my feet and frowned. 'I know your shoes are old and the children make fun of you. I will try to put another patch over the holes tonight after dinner. Now, go get washed up.'"

"I was so confused," Nana Emily told Lily. "Why couldn't she see my red shoes?" I went into my room and opened my school bag to pull out my old shoes, but they were gone. As the days went by, I came to understand that only I could see the beautiful red shoes."

Lily marveled at her grandma's story, thinking about
the red shoes. Just then, Nana Emily leaned over and pulled
off her warm, fuzzy, pink socks. Nana Emily wore those pink
socks all the time. In fact, Lily couldn't remember ever
seeing Nana Emily without those pink socks on her feet.

Lily could hardly believe her eyes. There,
on Nana's feet, were the red shiny shoes
with the word *Courage* written on them.

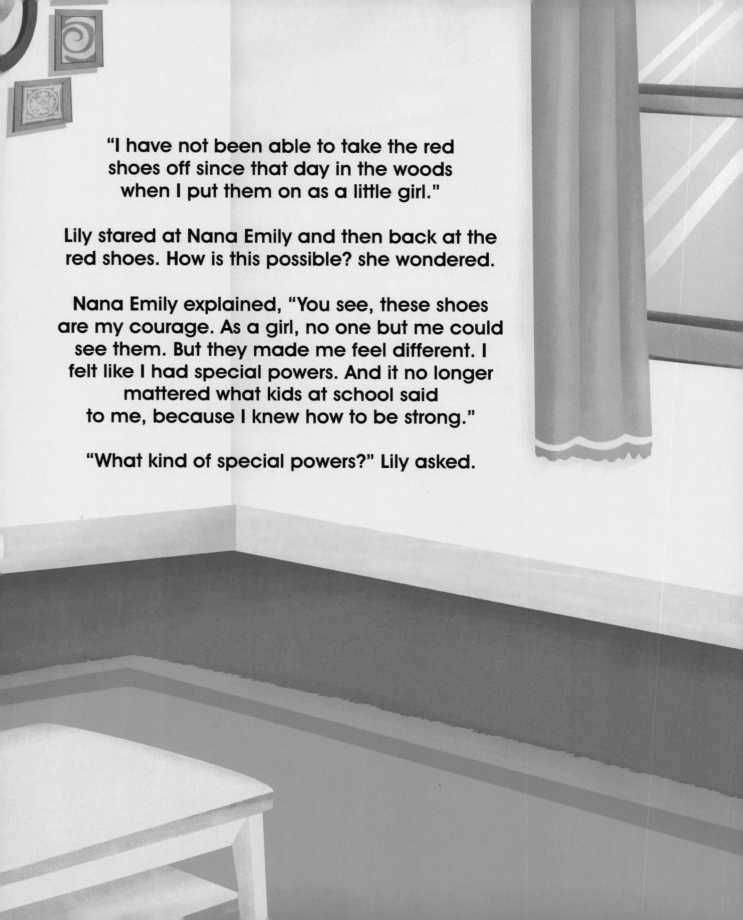

"I have not been able to take the red shoes off since that day in the woods when I put them on as a little girl."

Lily stared at Nana Emily and then back at the red shoes. How is this possible? she wondered.

Nana Emily explained, "You see, these shoes are my courage. As a girl, no one but me could see them. But they made me feel different. I felt like I had special powers. And it no longer mattered what kids at school said to me, because I knew how to be strong."

"What kind of special powers?" Lily asked.

Nana Emily smiled and hugged Lily. Then she reached over and gently took off Lily's school shoes, and she began to rub her feet. Lily smiled. She loved when Nana Emily rubbed her feet.

Then something magical happened. The beautiful, red shiny shoes with the sparkling gold words were now on Lily's feet!

Nana Emily's feet were once again covered with her pink fuzzy socks. She had tears in her eyes. "Why did you put the red shoes on my feet?" Lily asked.

Nana Emily answered, "Because, my sweet granddaughter, it is now your turn to wear the shoes of courage."

Lily looked down at her feet. She loved how beautiful they looked in the shiny red shoes. "What will happen now?" Lily asked.

Nana Emily squeezed her tightly and said, "The shoes will guide you."

Lily thought about the word courage. "Does it mean that if I wear these shoes, I will never be afraid?"

"No, Lily. Courage is not about never being afraid. It is a power inside of you that helps you do hard things even when you are afraid."

"Will they hurt?" Lily asked.

"Sometimes," Nana Emily said. "They can make you uncomfortable when you see that somebody is crying or scared.

There may even be times when you want to take the shoes off because it feels too hard to have courage.

Lily stared at her shoes and thought about courage. *What kind of things would she able to do if she only had courage?* she wondered.

Nana Emily hugged Lily. "Your shoes of courage will help you see things that you didn't see before.

You will hear what others say and understand their feelings better.

And sometimes your shoes will give you the greatest power of all— the superpower to stick up for other people."

The next day at school, Lily felt her feet tingling in her red shoes. She found Aleeza sitting by herself at lunch.

Lily took a deep breath and walked over to her.

"Hi, Aleeza I am sorry that I laughed when Molly made fun of your head scarf the other day. That was wrong," she said.

Aleeza looked sad. "Thank you, Lily. My feelings were really hurt. But you weren't the one who said mean things about my hijab, that's what my head scarf is called."

"But I laughed and didn't stick up for you," Lily replied.

"That is what my Nana Emily says is being a bystander— you know, somebody who watches other people treat people badly but won't help or say anything.

And I want to be an Upstander, someone who has courage and sticks up for other people even when it's hard."

Aleeza smiled and invited Lily to sit with her.

While they ate their lunch, Lily told Aleeza about Nana Emily and her white table. She invited Aleeza to bake treats with her at Nana Emily's house.

Nana Emily was very happy to meet Aleeza. She taught Aleeza how to make the dough and roll it out. Nana Emily dipped her fingers in the sugar bowl, licked them, and sang, "Yum, yum, not a crumb, on my thumb, diddly dum!" Then she let out a big burp. They all laughed.

The girls sat around the table with Nana Emily, eating sugar-coated fried dough, sharing stories, and laughing.

Aleeza told Nana Emily that Molly was the mean
girl at school. "She made fun of my hijab, and it felt
so awful," Aleeza said as she looked down at the table.

"When I wear my hijab it makes me feel close to God,"
Aleeza said. Lily smiled, "Oh, like I wear this cross on my neck.
It makes me feel close to God." The girls smiled at each other.

Nana Emily licked more sugar off her fingers and said, "I wonder why Molly is so mean."

The girls looked at each other.

Aleeza said, "Maybe she needs a friend?" Surprised, Lily looked at Aleeza and said, "But she has lots of friends!"

"Yes, but maybe she doesn't have any real friends who care about her," Aleeza said with a smile. "Maybe she is mean so she can get attention from people because she doesn't feel important," Nana Emily added.

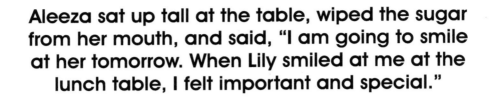

Aleeza sat up tall at the table, wiped the sugar from her mouth, and said, "I am going to smile at her tomorrow. When Lily smiled at me at the lunch table, I felt important and special."

Lily swung her feet under the chair. Her red shoes of courage were giving her an idea.

The next day at school, Lily went up to Molly.

Molly's face was red with anger. "What do you want? Why don't you go play with your friend with the stupid scarf," she yelled loudly, looking around and hoping that others heard her and were paying attention.

She wanted them to say mean things to Lily, too.

Lily took some sugar-coated fried dough out of her lunch box and handed it to Molly. "I know how much you like Nana Emily's treats, so I brought you one today," she said with a smile.

Molly looked confused. She wondered why Lily was being nice to her. Was it a trick?

"Why are you giving this to me?" Molly asked, unable to look Lily in the eye. "Because you are my friend," Lily answered with a smile.

"But, I was so mean to you," Molly said, staring at the ground.

"I know, and you were bullying Aleeza, which wasn't at all nice, but we all make mistakes. It is how we fix our mistakes that matters," Lily said, hearing Nana's voice in her head and feeling her strong, beautiful red shoes on her feet.

Molly followed Lily to the lunch table where Aleeza was sitting. She glanced at Aleeza and then quickly looked down at her hands and said, "I'm sorry for saying mean things about your hijab." Aleeza slowly smiled at Molly.

Lily clapped her hands and shouted,
" I know what the superpower is!"

Aleeza looked puzzled and asked,
"Superpower--like magical heroes have?"

"The superpower is called 'empathy',"
Lily said with a big smile.

"Empathy makes us strong, powerful and
able to do courageous things," explained Lily.

Lily smiled a bigger smile and said, "Empathy gave me the ability to imagine how embarrassed and alone you felt, Aleeza, when we laughed at your hijab, because I know how I feel when the boys and girls on my street make fun of me. I felt it with you."

"Yes," Molly said gently, "I understand the superpower of empathy. I can imagine how bad the things I said made all of you feel, because when my sister says mean things to me, I know how bad it makes me feel."

Lily's feet felt warm, cozy, and strong. She almost felt like her red shiny shoes had grown wings. She had never felt this powerful and confident before. She looked down at her shoes. But what she saw was something even more amazing!

The red shoes of courage were not only on her feet but also on the feet of her friends. They all had found the power of courage to feel what each other was feeling and to stand up for each other. They had been given the superpower of empathy.

Lily smiled when she realized that they would always be connected to each other because they had the courage to imagine how each other felt. They would never be alone.

They had become Upstanders.

CPSIA information can be obtained
at www.ICGtesting.com
Printed in the USA
LVHW071637210120
644286LV00004B/96